PUFFIN BOOKS

Published by the Penguin Group

Penguin Group (NZ), 67 Apollo Drive, Rosedale,
North Shore 0632, New Zealand (a division of Pearson New Zealand Ltd)
Penguin Group (USA) Inc., 375 Hudson Street,
New York, New York 10014, USA
Penguin Group (Canada), 90 Eglinton Avenue East, Suite 700, Toronto,
Ontario, M4P 2Y3, Canada (a division of Pearson Penguin Canada Inc.)
Penguin Books Ltd, 80 Strand, London, WC2R 0RL, England
Penguin Ireland, 25 St Stephen's Green,
Dublin 2, Ireland (a division of Penguin Books Ltd)
Penguin Group (Australia), 250 Camberwell Road, Camberwell,
Victoria 3124, Australia (a division of Pearson Australia Group Pty Ltd)
Penguin Books India Pvt Ltd, 11, Community Centre,
Panchsheel Park, New Delhi – 110 017, India
Penguin Books (South Africa) (Pty) Ltd, 24 Sturdee Avenue,
Rosebank, Johannesburg 2196, South Africa

Penguin Books Ltd, Registered Offices: 80 Strand, London, WC2R 0RL, England

First published by Penguin Group (NZ)
Published in Puffin Books, 2009
10 9 8 7 6 5 4 3 2 1

Designed by Book Design Ltd www.bookdesign.co.nz
Printed by Everbest Printing Co. Ltd, China

ISBN: 978 014 350350 7

A catalogue record for this book is available
from the National Library of New Zealand.

www.penguin.co.nz

Wheelbarrow Wilbur

Written by Narine Groome

Illustrated by Bevan Fidler

Wilbur the terrier was **cuddly** not fat,
a dog twice as big as your average cat.

Will owned the Abbotts,
as the Abbotts owned him –
Mum, Dad and Lucy, and best of all Tim.

The Abbotts went down to a new ice-cream shop, it wasn't so far, just a **skip** and a **hop**.

NOW Open
Ice Cream

Wilbur came too, to **frisk** with the strollers,
and **dance** from the reaches of incoming rollers.

He ran up the dunes, SLID down the slopes,

chased bouncing balls, snatched ends of ropes.

He **BARKED**
at the surfers,
escorted the boats,

rounded
up hats,
STOLE sneakers and coats.

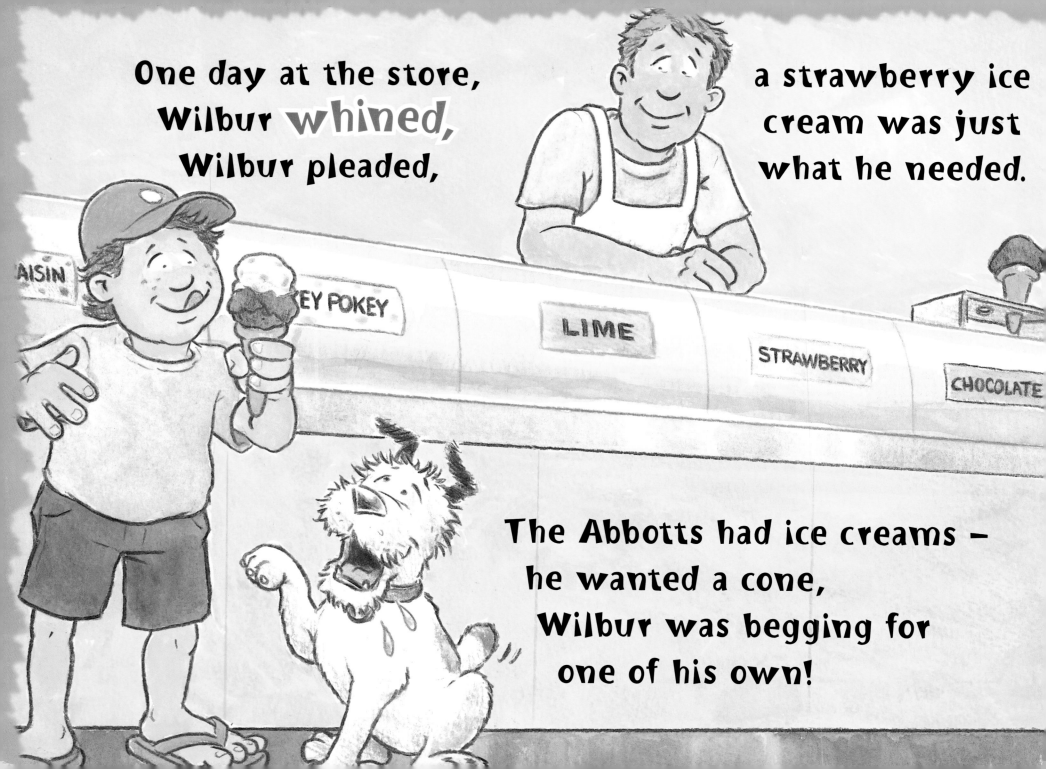

Tim bought him a cone with three flavours in it,

GOBBLE, GOBBLE, GULP –

gone in a minute.

And so it continued,
day after day,
Wilbur kept tucking
more ice creams away.

On barbeque nights
Wilbur sat by the table,
gulping up scraps
— all his tummy was able.

Sausages, potatoes
and slices of bread,
the Abbotts' dog
Wilbur was more
than well
fed!

And now ...

Waves caught and
bowled him,
rolled him
right up the beach,
because Wilbur, too fat,
couldn't dance out of reach.

He couldn't **steal** sunscreen,
or sneakers, or hats,
he couldn't **scare** seagulls,
race breakers, **chase** cats.

And still he ate ice creams
– completely extraneous,
all sizes, all flavours
– ice creams miscellaneous.

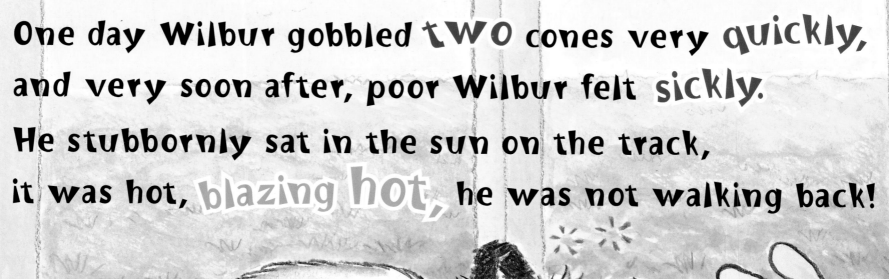

One day Wilbur gobbled **two** cones very quickly,
and very soon after, poor Wilbur felt sickly.
He stubbornly sat in the sun on the track,
it was hot, blazing **hot,** he was not walking back!

Tim tried to coax him but the dog wouldn't **budge,**
he was weighed down by ice cream,
hot chocolate . . . with fudge.

Tim fetched a barrow to push Wilbur back, bumping and **bouncing** along the **rough track**.

So into the barrow to the vet down the road,
went woebegone Wilbur, an unhappy load.

'What's this?' cried the vet.
'This dog's oversize!

Someone's been feeding him
ice cream and pies.

We'll fix your leg, Wilbur.
Let's give you injections,
to help with the pain and
prevent all infections.'

'This dog's leg is broken.
Operation and cast!'

Then away in a trolley
he whisked Wilbur fast,
saying, 'Wheelbarrow Wilbur,
you're simply too FAT.

We'll have to do something
at once about that.'

The Abbotts walked home
with instructions galore:

NO ice creams for Wilbur,
NO pies anymore.
NO sausages, potatoes,
scraps left by the cat,

PUBLIC → BEACH ACCESS

NO eating leftovers,
or unhealthy fat.

Wheelbarrow Wilbur began to grow thinner, at first the dog missed all the extras for dinner.

But he got lots of cuddles and kind strokes and pats, and people stopped by to have friendly chats.

Then back to the vet went Wheelbarrow Will,
in his cast made of plaster, he rode up the hill.
The vet freed his leg and said with a smile,
'You'll be good as new
in a very short while.'

And very soon ... Wilbur ran up the dunes, SLID down the slopes,

chased bouncing balls, snatched ends of ropes.

He **BARKED** at the surfers, escorted the boats,

rounded up hats, **fetched** sneakers and coats.

He **dashed** in and out of the legs of the strollers, **danced** out of reach of the incoming rollers.

Now Wheelbarrow Wilbur (who no longer begs),
is making good use of his own little legs.

No riding in barrows!
Will frolics with glee.

He's a trim dog, a slim dog,
as fit as can be.

And Will owns the Abbotts, as the Abbotts own him –
Mum, Dad and Lucy, and best of all Tim.

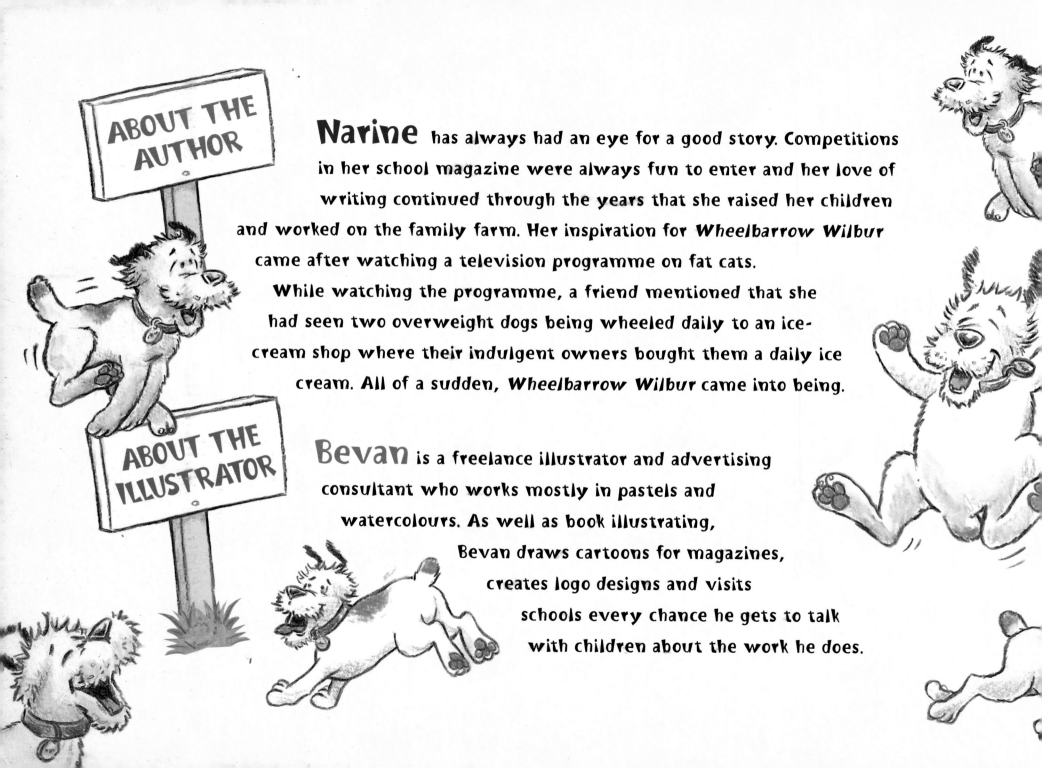

ABOUT THE AUTHOR

Narine has always had an eye for a good story. Competitions in her school magazine were always fun to enter and her love of writing continued through the years that she raised her children and worked on the family farm. Her inspiration for *Wheelbarrow Wilbur* came after watching a television programme on fat cats.

While watching the programme, a friend mentioned that she had seen two overweight dogs being wheeled daily to an ice-cream shop where their indulgent owners bought them a daily ice cream. All of a sudden, *Wheelbarrow Wilbur* came into being.

ABOUT THE ILLUSTRATOR

Bevan is a freelance illustrator and advertising consultant who works mostly in pastels and watercolours. As well as book illustrating, Bevan draws cartoons for magazines, creates logo designs and visits schools every chance he gets to talk with children about the work he does.